TALES
OF R.L. CULKIN
——————— VOL. 1

R.L. CULKIN

Copyright © 2023 R.L. Culkin.

All rights reserved. No part of this book may be reproduced, stored, or transmitted by any means—whether auditory, graphic, mechanical, or electronic—without written permission of both publisher and author, except in the case of brief excerpts used in critical articles and reviews. Unauthorized reproduction of any part of this work is illegal and is punishable by law.

ISBN: 979-8-89031-432-1 (sc)
ISBN: 979-8-89031-433-8 (hc)
ISBN: 979-8-89031-434-5 (e)

Because of the dynamic nature of the Internet, any web addresses or links contained in this book may have changed since publication and may no longer be valid. The views expressed in this work are solely those of the author and do not necessarily reflect the views of the publisher, and the publisher hereby disclaims any responsibility for them.

One Galleria Blvd., Suite 1900, Metairie, LA 70001
(504) 702-6708
1-888-421-2397

THE LIGHT OF GIA PANTA

In the afterlife, there is a world that reaches the end of the universe. In this world, there is every creature, being, sentient, computer, cyborg, demon, and entity of life that you have never even imagined. The forces of light have vast civilizations that lie in every corner of the universe but in between the patches of light there is dark and there is far more dark than light. In the dark, there are foes with power unimaginable to that of the common spirit. In the world of the dead, the world that they call Gia Panta. In this world, a person gets infinite lives like a cheat code in a video game. The only catch is that your spirit starts from your dwelling or your house which is in fact like a spiritual spawning point. There are no save points along the way and you have to re-travel that distance to get to where you died. You also have levels like in a video game which is mostly time-based. It is also based on what you did in life so if you had a craft, you did all of your life you start at a higher level than someone who did the same job for less time. You can learn new skills in Gia Panta but you will always have the skills you learned in life and you can grow the skills you had in life to potentials unimaginable.

There has been a war in Gia Panta since the light came to be. In this war, there are two kinds of soldiers good and bad unless you count the free souls, people that were granted the ability to travel between the realms of dark and light. For you see that soul from the light can go into the dark whenever they chose. Souls that dwell in the dark are vanquished to the dark for all time unless they can distinguish the light and Bring Gia Panta to the rules of before time when dark was all there was. The force that is free to travel back and forth has to follow the laws of both the light and the dark thus leaving some of the free souls to be barred from the light parts of Gia Panta. In this group of souls, there is a small group of warriors that have banded together for protection from the things of the dark. They are usually found in camp on the outskirts of the light but the Angel guard usually pushes them out to just beyond where the reaches of the light show.

The war has taken its toll on the light and they are running low on soldiers. Eldon the king of the light and the knower of all feels that he has no choice but to call in the leader of the free souls General Skull. An x military special force general became a free soul based on a wish granted to him by the celestial council. He and his soldiers have lived in the dark for millenniums and have faced almost everything the dark has to offer. They also have enchanted weapons that kill creatures of the dark faster than any weapon that the light has. To spread infinite light threw the dark they will need the help of General Skull.

A rider sits atop a white unicorn with a magenta hooded cloak and armor that shines in the light. In the shadow of the cloak, you can see a slight outline of a face and two white glowing eyes peering through the darkness. Soon all you see is the rider's two eyes. The rider ventures further into the darkness. He comes across a fire in the distance. The rider approaches the fire with caution. He dismounts his unicorn and creeps closer to the camp. Soon he is in a hiding place that he can see from. He peers out to the fire and notices that he has walked into a camp of Borlocks pig-headed men creatures who feast on the souls of the light.

The rider carefully yet hastily goes back to his unicorn to flee but just as he gets there he is seen by a youngling. The youngling sounds the alarm. "Fresh meat! Me like Fresh meat! get them me hungry." yelled the youngling.

Soon there were three adult Borlocks on steeds of Cerberus hell hounds coming riding after the rider with the white glowing eyes. So, the rider with the white glowing eyes looks back to see only one Borlock behind him. Then he senses that he is in trouble he has lost two of the borlocks and has no idea how to get back to the light. Soon he comes to a ridge in the dark. One of the Borlocks a top of his Cerberus jumps out from the ridge. The rider with the white glowing eyes tries to go the other way but there too stands a Borlock a top of a Cerberus. Soon the rider with the white glowing eyes is surrounded by three hungry Borlocks a top Cerberus hell hounds.

"Ummm! Good! The human spirit and unicorn. We eat well tonight!" grunts the main Borlock of the group as the side of its face comes flying off in little pieces and chunks of its skull and splatter of bone and neon green glowing blood. Then a barrage of bangs and explosions coming from the darkness take out the two remaining Borlocks and all three Cerberus hell hounds. The smoke clears and left atop the unicorn sits the rider with the white glowing eyes. "Who goes there?" asks the rider.

A man with a thick dark beard that fell to his stomach and dark brown eyes almost black wearing stealth black camouflage and a bulletproof vest that has the symbol of a red X across his chest on his belt a belt buckle with the skull of a baby demon on it. He has a strong build and is about 6 Ft tall. It is a general Skull. "Who dare venture into these parts alone?" replied General Skull.

"It is I Kalamtha the messenger of the holy royal lord himself sent to ask the duties of General Skull and his Darkness Ranger Army of the free souls." announced the rider Kalamtha.

"What the hell does His holiness need my help for further why should I help him?" growled General Skull.

"a full pardon to you and all your banished soldiers as well as another wish of your choice of course," answered Kalamtha.

"What do you think boys and girls should we go back to the light and help his lordship?" yelled General Skull to his men.

"YEAH!" Yelled the Darkness Rangers about 200 strong.

A light showed down to Kalamtha and a path of light appeared. Kalamtha leads the solder to the lands of the light. When they arrive, they see a vast city just as far as the eye could see. Everything was busy all the spirits just floating around going about their wondrous after lives it seemed as busy as a bee hive to the Darkness Rangers who have lived in camps in the dark for millennium because they were banished for breaking the laws of the light. They were joyous to see paradise once again.

Their soldiers were led to the new royal Dwellings and Kalamtha led General Skull to the Royal Lord Eldon. The two walk through the royal hall and head toward the throne of the Royal Lord Eldon as he sits with silver colored beard and hair that drags the ground Smokey Grey eyes and a perfect physique.

Wearing a purple toga and bare feet. Besides him was his staff of knowledge which allows him to know all. they approach the Royal lord Kalamtha kneel to his lord and urge General Skull to do the same and slowly He does. "I bring you here to ask for your help to vanquish the leader of the dark force him and his generals there are 7 of them and they are the head of the dark forces kill them and the dark army has no one to lead it. We would do this but I need my best warriors here to protect the light and that is why I need you." beaconed Royal Lord Eldon.

"I'll need three things from you and I think you know what it is… I need my three best men who have been housed in a prison of the light for as long as I have been banished to the dark. Know if I can't have them the no deal!" taunted General Skull.

"I'll Have you and your men sent to prison. how would you and your people like that?" warned Royal Lord Eldon.

"Just fine actually at least they will get food and water!" remarked General Skull.

"I must ponder this I will send for you on whether you go to prison or whether Dragon Jake, Walker Cloud, and Sammie the Maton will be released into your care. Now leave me." rambled the Royal Lord.

General Skull heads back to his new royal Dwelling and wonders how long is he going to be in paradise and if he does take the mission what will he and his Darkness Rangers face he knows they won't all come back because when a free soul dies in the darkness they now belong to the dark. They will still have infinite life but they must from that point on serve the dark.

The Royal Lord sits in front of the Royal Council. "We must free some of the light's worst criminals and I think it is far past due. Besides it is better to have them on our side rather than inoperable." bargained the Royal Lord.

"These three individual souls destroyed countless city blocks hurt hundreds of innocent souls as well as the smuggling of illicit substances. And on top of all that they've desecrated one of our most sacred shrines." argued the councilwoman.

"Yes but no one was killed!" replied the Royal Lord.

"That's beside the point the souls are the scum of our world and cannot be set free. Furthermore..." said the councilwoman as she was interrupted by the Royal Lord.

"That is not what they are. It's just their life skills are bad ones it just means that they will be better equipped to handle the leader of the Dark." urged the Royal Lord.'

"We will allow it the council has ruled 2 to 1." said a councilman.

CHAPTER

In a dark concrete cell on the floor lays a man with long blonde hair and a long full beard, light blue eyes a pointy nose, and a medium size build. In a cell next to him also dark a man sits in a bed with round-shaped glasses and long brown hair and brown eyes and a large build. In the cell next to him tucked away in the corner is a man with a very long mustache and goatee. Brown eyes and dark brown hair. He has tattoos on his face and a scar on his left eye. The first is Dragon Jake and the Second is Cloud Walker and the Third Is Sammie the Maton or Sammie the Thug and they all served time in the special force with General Skull. The only problem is they get rowdy when they're together and they all have tremendously high Life levels and have been honing their skill for millenniums, suffice it to say they are mostly bad skills they are still good souls.

The door to the three men's cell opens and they are all three blinded by the light. "you three are free to go courtesy of General Skull but you can't unsheathe your weapons until you leave the reaches of the light. The three men strong from working out and not wearing their shirts step out of the cells. They go through the process and are brought to their new royal dwellings. They are given new royal garb. They are brought to a room in the royal castle with a table and at the end of it are General Skull and his new right-hand woman Tenshi. The three men are elated to see their old friend and rejoice. Soon there is a feast and festivities. The General urges his soldier to have a merry time for soon they ride.

General Skull walks away from the party and goes to talk with Royal Lord Eldon. "Royal Lord we will need supplies and prevision for the trip into the darkness. Also, we will need all the intelligence you have on these dark generals and this Lord of the Darkness. What is his name by the way?" blurted General Skull.

"You will have your supplies and previsions but your weapon fare much better than the weapons of the light! And his name is Contra" stated the Royal Lord Eldon.

"I didn't say I needed weapons. Our weapon sends all the monsters running. But that is because they were made by the dark to kill the dark. You can't be just anyone you have to have killed in life to yield one of these weapons and all my men and women have. Now that's not something we're proud of but that's the one thing that will get us through this and that's the one thing we got on you." growled General Skull.

"Very well then you leave in two-time cycles. Get your men ready and I will have all you request.

Also, you will get your next wish if and when you come back!?" sneered the Royal Lord Eldon.

"You say that Like it's not gone Happens. Do not worry me and my soldiers have been missing this place it's paradise and we ain't gone take it for granted again," replied General Skull.

"Very well!" replied the Royal Lord Eldon.

The time has come for the General and his men to go on their great adventure to the Darkness they are the Darkness Rangers after all. The men are given unicorns, griffins, and Pegasus for their travels as well as a centaur to carry and guard the supplies and provisions. Once the soldiers leaves on their adventure they will be on their own beside the owls that fly by night and can see in the darkness to deliver messages back and forth. As they get ready to leave the Royal Lord Eldon hands a map and scroll to General Skull. "This is all the intelligence we have on the Dark, a map and a magic scroll just ask it a question and it will generate a reply in purple ink." warned the Royal Lord Eldon.

The Darkness Rangers are off to battle. They head down the main boulevard as the spirits wave and cheer for them and soon they are in the outreaches of the light and they begin their mission. The general gets his bearings and pulls out his map. He looks at it and pulls out his compass of truth, it always tells the true direction that a soul is traveling. The General set his course. And the soldiers are off. The General his three best friends and his Number One Tenshi.

CHAPTER

The soldiers press on in the darkness and comes to a river of fire. The general sends men ahead on the Pegasus to see what is past the river while he and the men find a way across the river. Soon the ground shakes and the soldiers are shaken. Then out from the river comes the head of a worm an elder dragon spitting fire and trying to eat the Darkness Rangers. The Darkness Rangers take cover and begin to fight the Worm. The General and his captains Walker, Sammie, Jake, and Tenshi retreat to a ridge and watch the Rangers take formation and fight and advance on the Worm. Soon the worm is overwhelmed and the creature falls. The Ranger cut out its heart to make sure. The battle is over and the fire worm's dead body turns into a hard carbon substance petrified in its death pose, which just so happens to be a perfect bridge for him and his men to get across the river of fire and they do cross.

Soon the scouts on the Pegasus are back to report an army of orcs and goblins. They are about 10,000 deep and they are camped out for 5 clicks in all directions. The General and his four captains have a war council. "How can we fight through these fucks? There is no way. And even if we do, we'll lose too many men." barked General Skull.

"Then we go around!" remarked Tenshi.

"Yeah, but that will take us two-time cycles of course" interjected Dragon Jake.

"Yeah, but we will all be alive or have you forgotten that if you die in the dark as a free soul then you become that of the dark," stated General Skull.

"So, I haven't forgotten I've just been utterly hopeless until I got out of that goddamn cell and 10,000 orcs and goblins don't scare me one bit!" stated Dragon Jake.

"You fuck! And that's why you're here you fear nothing but this time we ain't gone use muscle we gone use our brains and go around" ordered Skull.

The Darkness rangers travel for five clicks and on the last click are spotted by a goblin scout. He blows the horn and sounds the alarm. Soon the ground is shaking from the running march of the orcs and goblins. The sky is flooded by the flight of dragons and their riders the heckling banshee lord's evil fucker that will suck your life force from you in a draw of their breath and their screams will paralyze you if you're too close. "Send out scouts for the first hiding spot you can find and get me the SEALs snipers we need to take out those fucking Banshee! Tell everyone to go live on hellfire round let's take these fucks down!" ordered the General.

The five SEALs in the group head for high ground with their rifles and scopes and plenty of hellfire bullets made from gold 24-carat. Useless in paradise but all the monster seems to hoard because a dark creature is allergic to it if it enters the bloodstream they will be poisoned to death and they've got lots of ammo and plenty of gold to make into bullets. Soon the banshee lords are in sight and the SEALs are also in position. The SEALs signal the General and he signals back. There are 7 Banshee lords and the SEALs put on their suppressors on their rifles and disappear with invisibility camo. The banshee lord draws closer and you see five flashes come from the ridge where the seals are and then the back of five banshee lord heads get scattered all over the sky. The other two banshee lords start to scream. Two more flashes and this time it's the tops of the banshee lord's heads that get scattered through the air with a mist of green glowing blood. "What took so long?" Radioed the General to the SEALs.

"We were fighting over who gets to kill those fuckers' sir!" radioed the SEALs.

"Well, that's good shooting soldiers be on alert!" ordered the captain.

The scouts are back and they report an old temple that could hide the force about a click and a half away. The General orders his men to rendezvous at the temple. He thought to himself we should just make it, but those monsters are fast we must hurry.

The soldiers come to the temple which is made from a black stone and is Asian in architecture. It is just big enough for him and his Rangers. "Load up in the temple and bunker down till those orcs and goblins pass no fires and be quiet!" rifled the General in a hurry. The Rangers take shelter and the General pulls out his map. He realizes that he is now close to the dead path which will take them to the forest of the forsaken but they will have to cross the backbone path.

The rumbling of the orcs and goblins grows close until it just stops. The General looks out threw his periscope. All he could see were dark figures with red glowing eyes just standing there like there was some force keeping them from crossing onto the temple grounds. A horn sound and the army of orcs and goblins turns around and leaves with the rumble of their march getting quieter and quieter. And then a voice Beaconed all around. "Who dares enter the temple of the dishonorable samurai? All the men and women have too much honor to take refuge in my temple. Leave now or die by the hand of my blade!" said the voice in a heavy sound that echoed.

"We will leave in a hurry we do not want trouble if you will let us pass, we will be gone!" yelled the General to the voice.

That woman by your side has a good physic if she can land one attack against my blade Chi Ga Nusumu then I will let you pass." beaconed the voice.

"I will kill you! You dishonorable samurai." taunted Tenshi before the General could stop her.

"Do you know who I am I am the greatest samurai that ever lived Subarashi Mono and I am the slayer of an army who earned the title of dishonorable for killing my emperor's army because he took my wife and when he was done with her, she was hanged and, in my anger, and passion I killed 20,000 troops and the emperor himself only to be killed by the emperor's wife with a dagger to the back. The dark arose this temple in the dishonor that I committed by killing all those men. Your challenge has been excepted." snarled Subarashi Mono.

The samurai appeared in the middle of the group wearing golden samurai armor and his Katana Chi Ga Nusumu is about eight feet long. He puts his hands together and begins his katas. A hora of red grows bigger and bigger around him. "Let's give them room boys" ordered the general as the Rangers make a ring out of their bodies by making a big circle. Tenshi enters an average size woman with long black hair that flows below her butt. Ample breasts and a tight well-conditioned body. A round pretty face with wide brown eyes and a cute button nose. She pulls her Katana and raises it for battle.

CHAPTER

Subarashi Mono raises his eight-foot katana and the battle begins. Subarashi Mono charges Tenshi and as soon as he is in range attacks. One swing, two swings, and three but his attack is evaded every time. Subarashi Mono is getting frustrated. Then Subarashi Mono makes a fatal mistake as he charges and overextends his swing and leaves his ribs exposed. Tenshi throws a wicked knee to the ribs of Subarashi Mono, he is stunted for a brief moment. That's when Tenshi takes advantage, she strikes with her katana stabbing the hand that controls Subarashi Mono's sword.

Subarashi Mono bows in defeat. "For your test, you have done the utmost. I will grant you the aid of Chi Ga Nusumu. This sword has its own soul but I cannot wield it for I am not the best samurai anymore. Lord Tenshi of the Darkness Rangers I present to you Chi Ga Nusumu wield it with honor. Also, do not sheath the sword or it will grow angered for being trapped and will thirst for battle and innocent souls." explained Subarashi Mono.

Tenshi bowed to Subarashi Mono as she took the sword from him and then the sword shortened to six feet and just magically holstered is self on the back of Tenshi. "That sword will automatically morph to fit its master so fight with much Honor as for me I will now become a priest of the dark and train my aikido to one day battle you again for the right to Chi Ga Nusumu," remarked Subarashi Mono.

The Rangers and General Skull are granted passage to the path that will take them to Backbone Pass and into the forest of the forsaken. The soldiers head out "You know Tenshi, I wish you wouldn't fight in such big battles without my permission greatest samurai in Gia Panta." muttered General Skull to Tenshi quietly.

Soon the Rangers came to backbone Pass. It got really cold and the wind was making it colder. The General ordered the men to set up camp at the bottom of the pass. The soldier set up camp and assess the area for the best way to get over the pass with the unicorns. The widest point on the pass is only 3 feet wide. The General knows that if they let them go, they will run nonstop until they reach their stable but that will add 7-time cycles to the trip. The General ponders the conundrum.

The General knowing that the wind and cold are never going to stop decides not to let the unicorns run back to their stables and take his chances. The Rangers pack up camp and start their journey again. It takes them the whole time cycle to cross the Backbone pass but when they get over it, they are relieved. They start their descent into the forest of the forsaken and the first thing you see is the souls of the forsaken hanging from the trees by their necks, trying to get out but they can't. The further they travel into the forest the more uncomfortable they become. Soon the path brings them to a wall. On the wall, there is a riddle, a thing that breathes smoke and fire and has the hide of armor, answer this and be in woe but if defeated then threw the gate you will go.

Everyone racks their brains trying to figure out what it is. Then Dragon Jake gets it in his head. "it's a dragon that's what breaths smoke and fire and has the hide of armor." realizes Dragon Jake.

Then a gate appears in front of the army. They all cheer. Then the General begins to think about the part that said in woe and as the gate swung open a Black dragon spit's a Fire acid into the Rangers standing in front of the gate. "Take cover!" ordered General Skull.

The rangers take cover and begin to fight the Dragon. The fight goes back and forth. There are more casualties from the ranger. Soon Chi Ga Nusumu starts glowing and vibrating. The dragon senses the sword and stops his assault. "Chi Ga Nusumu? How could the world's greatest samurai be with these ragtag soldiers? Show yourself, wielder of Chi Ga Nusumu." Bellowed the dragon.

Tenshi steps out of the cover of a big rock. "But that is not Subarashi Mono! Who are you and what has become of Subarashi Mono?" asked the dragon.

The General explained how they must stop the lord of Darkness Contra and that Subarashi was not killed only hit and how he gave up the sword with honor. The Dragon is neutral to the side of dark or light and said that if they part with some gold, they will be able to pass. And the Dragon assures them that the men that died will be treated the best they can for being part of the dark now. But since the Dragon killed them, they will be his Souls and he vows they will not have to suffer.

The Soldiers honor their dead and give the Dragon the gold. They head further into the forest and soon it becomes hot and humid. The Rangers and General Skull set up camp for the night. In about three Time cycles they will be on the front lines of the Contra army and the real battles will take place.

The Darkness Rangers head out to the destination. Soon they reach a cliff, below the cliff is the light of what looks to be hundreds of thousands deep. Fire pits are burning and in the background a Dark Castle atop a dark mountain. The sky glows red with fire and smoke. General Skull knowing that he and his soldiers will never get through the hordes of dark soldiers decides to sneak around the force. He knows this will take far longer but there is no other way.

General Skull splits his men and women into four groups and gives the command to his captains Cloud, Jake, and Sammie and Tenshi will go with his group. He instructs them to all take different routes to the castle and regroup at the bottom of the gate. The groups set out on their mission.

THE BOOK OF CLOUD WALKER

Cloud and his soldiers take a long way around to the back gate of the palace and hope to bring the element of surprise. Along the path in the dark the crunch of bones underfoot and the smell of flesh burning. As the troops head North along the path. Soon the path narrows and they have to find their way on foot from here out so they send their unicorns home although they know that this deep in that they are food for some evil entity. On their right is a wall of black ice that rises as high as the eye can see. On the other side, there is a cliff and a drop to the dark valley where all sorts of dark creatures dwell. They walk along the path with several close calls of men almost falling to their demise but a last come to a ruin of a tall cylindrical tower, at the top a weird symbol of the dark that had not been seen for millenniums, with an inscription that reads "do not trust the creatures of this land for they will eat your soul with tricks and you will dwell in torment in the gut of the creature forever." this is bad because no one in the group can read this inscription.

Cloud and his group press on only to find the ruins of what looks to be a once thriving town. They walk through its empty street and it is weary how quiet it is. Then they hear a child scream. Cloud threw up his hand and give orders to his men to spread out and seek out the problem, with hand signals. The 48 darkness rangers spread out into eight teams of six rangers and all take different routes to where they all heard the scream.

The first team to arrive on the scene team Cobra and all they see is an empty street. Soon all the Darkness Rangers converge on the location and when they get there, there is nothing, and then all of a sudden walls fall from the ruins up above and the creatures of this dark land come out. The creatures outnumber and would overwhelm the Darkness Rangers so they are put in a tight position should they try and shoot their way out or back down?

Captain Cloud Decides to be civil and bargain his way out and if that does not work then he'll blast his way out. A midsize slimy creature with a big mouth and sharp teeth and long skinny arms that drag the ground and a head with no neck they have grey skin festering with puss-filled blisters and short stumpy legs holding up bean shape body with fowl-smelling guts of fat holding wicked spears with twisted, spiny, sharp metal tips.

Out from the tallest ruin stepped out of the shadow a big version of the creature. All of the other creatures make weird and horrifying noises the big one lets out a roar. There is silence. "Why should I let you and your men pass through my part of the darkness?" bellowed the main creature.

"Forgive me we were not able to go the other way and thought this a barren land with no inhabitants," replied Cloud.

"What is your business in these realms as us Gromits have not seen another soul for millenniums?" asked the Gromit King.

"It is not something I can dispose to you!" replied Cloud.

"Are you prepared to fight for some simple information? I promise that we will not tell anyone for you are the first soul we have come across in millenniums and we would love to have you." snickered The Gromit King.

"What do you mean have us?" asked Cloud

"Umm… I meant Help you." said the Gromit King coyly.

"Just lead us to the path out of here and we will be on our way," replied Cloud.

"I shall show you after a party in your honor." snarled the Gromit King.

"I must pass as we must make it to our destination post haste." retorted Cloud.

"Answer me this question and I will let you pass if not we will feast on your souls." sneered the Gromit King.

"It would come to that… fuck!" blurted Cloud.

"What is greater than god and eviler that the darkest demon?" Remarked the Gromit King. Cloud thought to himself and he was drawing a blank. All of the Darkness Rangers stand behind Captain Cloud ready to strike out if they have to. Cloud still thinking to himself "NOTHING!" yelled Cloud.

The army of Gromits gasped. The King of the Gromits raised his hand and they were silent again. "In all the time I have lived I have never had the honor of being witness to someone who got the riddle right, which is why I hate to devour your souls anyway!" growled the Gromit King.

"Seize them!" yelled one of the other Gromits

"All right boys we got creeps coming in hot get me a scout team and blow me a fuckin' path through these filthy fucks and do with a vengeance!" remarked Captain Cloud.

"Sir Yes Sir! You heard him boys let's give 'em hell!" ordered the next in command.

Captain Cloud and his men started to fire hellfire bullets at the Gromits easily killing them soon they heard the blast of the hellfire bombs clearing a path out of there. Captain Cloud orders his men to get out and take as many of the things out as they can. The soldiers run through the ruins of the town being swarmed by Gromits. Two soldiers are taken out and devoured by the Gromits. Soon the Darkness rangers come to the edge of the town and they see nothing but dark thorny tall dead trees as far as the eyes can see. And amid the thorns a small unworn path. The men head into the forest.

The captain and his men thinking they are safe head deeper into the forest and they start to hear whispering. At first, they think it's just them but soon they hear laughing which soon thereafter turns into screaming. Soon the screaming is unbearable. The men cover their ears to muffle the sound but it is no use. They all start to run on the path away from the shrieking only to come to a three-way fork in the road. On the side of either path, there is a giant old dead tree. The men are hesitant and just pick the first path that seems best and two men run to the left path only to be torn to pieces and devoured by the branches of the tree. Another man runs to the path on the right and gets his head bitten off by one of the branches as others tear his body apart and feed on it. The shrieking still going on Captain Cloud orders them through the middle path and surprisingly nothing happened. The captain and his soldiers ran for a long time until they came to a dry river bed and soon the screaming stopped.

As the Captain and his men come to a ridge, they see that they are closer than they thought and can see the Dark Lord Contra's Palace. The Darkness Rangers press on thinking that they have the element of surprise but they have been spotted by an evil enchanter in the tower high above the palace. The enchanter goes and tells the Dark lord Contra and they decide to lay in wait and take only the captain alive and to kill the rest.

Soon the Darkness Rangers make it to the back gate. Cloud thinks to himself is this a trap? But thinks it is a second too late and a battle ensues. The Darkness Rangers fight well for a while but soon are overwhelmed by the unrelenting forces. All of the solder huddle around Captain Cloud and slowly one by one Captain Cloud's team of darkness ranger parish only to become a soldier of the enemy. Cloud is left standing covered in blood "COME ON YOU FUCKS! KILL ME TOO! KILL ME TOO…" cried Cloud as soldiers of the dark move in slowly and capture him as he puts up a fight and is soon thereafter subdued. He is taken to the dungeon.

THE BOOK OF JAKE THE DRAGON SLAYER

Captain Jake and his men stay back and set up camp. Their job is to provide backup for the other three captains if needed. After setting up camp Captain Jake sends out a scout team for some intel on the positions of troops and artilleries things of that nature. He also sends out troops to put up traps with light bombs and hellfire mines.

The troop head out on their mission. The scouts find a ridge where they can spot all of the dark army and the position of almost everything they need to know. Also, they can see the Dark Palace from here and can assess strategies to take the whole place out with one strike. They have done their mission and are on their way back.

The trapped crew also sets up some explosives and puts them all along the path. They make it so there is one way in and one way out. All other ways are booby-trapped. They head back to the camp to get some R&R.

Back at the camp, things are as good as they can be. There is fire to keep them warm food to eat and some drink to have. The soldiers takes president for this may be their last fun before they die.

Some time has passed and a messenger from General Skulls Group shows up at the camp and informs Captain Jake that they need help. The captain orders the men to start packing. The messenger tells Jake that they got deep into the forces of the dark army and even took a post which is where they are held up now. But they got pinned down and need some backup to clear a path and provide cover.

Jake and his troops are finished packing "This is it boys you may not come back a free soul but you will always be one of General Skulls Darkness Rangers And remember that!" urged Captain Jake.

"Wait! Wait! Captain Jake Wait." yelled a new messenger from Captain Sammie's Group.

"Halt!" yelled Captain Jake.

The new messenger tells the captain that they are pinned down with their back to a wall and need reinforcements to take a side gate that is strategically flawed and can be the way in to kill the Dark Lord Contra. Captain Jake Decides to split his men in half 24 men in each group and he will go to the aid of the General. The orders are made and the two now smaller groups now head off in different directions.

When Jake and his team get to the location the battle is raging. The soldiers signal that they are ready to take the gate. General Skull and his group signal for them to hold on until they give the signal. On his throne in the tower watching the battle play out "have the General and his Captains captured and put them in the dungeon with their comrade Cloud." Ordered Dark Lord Contra.

The General signals for Captain Jake to make his move and head for the main gate while the General's men give them cover. Jake and his men move in and are making ground on the gate. General Skull and his men are giving them cover fire and doing a damn good job at it. Soon Captain Jake and his men are on top of the gate, with cover fire they defeat the last of the guards to have the gate open to 10,000 soldiers lying in wait "Oh Shit..." remarked Captain Jake.

Jake ordered his men to retreat to the post that the General was holding down but it was futile and the dark soldiers killed all his Darkness Rangers and takes him captive. Meanwhile, all the General can do is watch and hope that they can hold off the massive army with just Him, Tenshi, and about 30 Darkness Rangers. He thought to himself retreat or fight and at that moment, he thought to fight.

THE BOOK OF SAMMIE

Captain Sammie and his darkness rangers take the long and grueling mountain pass. Their route is the longest and most dangerous but will be the most likely to be undetected. Along the journey, they see the giant acid- spitting dragons that patrol the skies with their lich riders on their backs. You could also look out at the dark palace and the souls that fly across the dark skies into the high tower of the dark palace where they get their task in the afterlife. Down below a metropolis of army camps with fires lighting the ground like the lights of L.A. an ancient city that once stood.

Sammie and his men pushed on and they walked on the bones of the dead. Soon they will have to climb treacherous paths with sharp jagged rock. One soldier jumps to a hold and loses his fingers and falls to his death. Sammie orders his men to go slow and soon they are at the summit of Black Mountain. The descent into a valley takes him and his Darkness Rangers to the back gate of the palace. Soon the men approach the gate and take out the guards only to be spotted by a Lich and his acid-spitting dragon. "Fall back to the mountain back there and keep your backs to the wall. Take out these fucks but try to conserve ammo!" barked out Sammie

"YES SIR!" yelled the Rangers.

"I need someone to go back to the camp and get reinforcements any spetnas in the group?" yelled Sammie.

"Sir yes Sir!" spoke the only spetna of the group.

"You some tuff fucking bastards, we went up against you in old WWIII… well get back to that base ASAP solder we can't be wasting time!" bellowed Sammie.

All the rest of the Darkness Rangers stay and fight with the dark army at the back gate. They have the advantage and will kill the dark army soldier but they just keep coming out of the woodwork. "I need two green berets to sneak into the palace and get Intel on anything you can find out and then bring it back to me!" Ordered Sammie.

The two soldiers head to find a way in without being detected. They come to a small drainage ditch and decide to follow it in and it leads to the bowels of the Dark Palace. They make their way through the labyrinth of tunnels and end up coming out in the dungeon. As they sneak by the cells, they hear a whisper and when they turned to see who it was it was General Skull, Jake the Dragon Slayer, Cloud Walker, and Tenshi. "Wow you guys look to be in some trouble?" asked one of the green berets.

"Oh, we're fine just get some reinforcement and we will be waiting for the calvarias. Now go!" said General Skull.

Sammie and his Darkness Rangers hold down the position indefinitely and soon the Scouts that braved going into the Dark Palace came back with info that show a good breach point with explosives and a chink in the armor so to speak. He also informed Captain Sammie that the General and the Other Captains are in the dungeon and that once the wall is breached, they will take the shortest path to the Dungeon.

Just about that time the backup arrives and Sammie poses a bold move to keep the gate occupied and sends a group to the dark palace breach point and hit 'em hard from two spots. They set out on their mission while about 15 Darkness Rangers stay behind to keep the gate occupied, while the rest of the rangers go to the breach point. Soon it will be no turning back do or die.

THE PATH OF THE GENERAL

General Skull Tenshi and his Darkness Rangers must take the hardest path of all, straight into the heart of the monsters. It would most likely end in death but they must try or it is the end of the light in the entire universe. Air dropped is all the heavy artillery from the wars of the people of the earth like jeeps with 50 cal. Machine guns mounted to them and hummers as well as 4 tanks and 6 Mechs from the Dudiron era. And 1 stealth bomber with two stealth fighter jets to keep him company and various other heavy artillery. The soldier head toward the dark palace.

The General and his men are met by the Dark Forces and the fight ensues. Looking from the view of the General there was nothing but a dark force for light years ahead "Light em' up boys and let's try to give some cover to the Golden Eagle O.K. Falcon one and two!" ordered General Skull to the Planes in the air.

Immediately there are dragons with lich riders and they are about 12 strong. The fighter jet breaks away from the stealth bomber as it rises to a light bomb-safe altitude. If they can drop the bomb, they will almost be done they will just have to take key points to take the dark and bring forth the light. As the bomber goes up there is a dragon that follows him up as the rest of the dragons go after the fighter jets. There is a great dogfight between the dragons and the fighter jets and the jets take out all but two of the dragons before getting shot down themselves. The stealth bomber drops the mega light bomb and then another but one of the bombs is taken out by the flame of the dragon that followed him before the stealth bomber can dodge the dragon's flame it too gets taken out but one of the bombs is a direct hit.

Even though it was a direct hit it was only enough to clear half of the path. The general and his men move forward but take heavy fire from the dark forces. Soon the tanks get taken out and then the Mechs fall, and they keep falling until it is just Tenshi and the General. The lich and the dragon land in front of the General and Tenshi who is wildly yielding her katana "Take them to the dungeon and bring me that sword it will be my new weapon." hissed the Lich.

The dark soldiers go and tie up the General and Tenshi and they take the sword and wrap it in a temporary sheath and they set out for the dungeon. Tenshi and General Skull are thrown into a cell with Cloud Walker Dan and Jake the dragon Slayer "Fancy seeing you here I guess now are only hope is Sammie then?" blasted Jake.

"He can do it," stated Skull

Just then they heard the voice of one of the green barrettes "Hey General you guys need some help?" whispered the green barrette.

"We're just waiting on the Calvary so do your jobs we will be fine," orders General Skull.

CHAPTER

"GET ME OUT OF HERE! GET ME OUT! I CAN'T TAKE IT!" screams Tenshi's sword as it sends an energy wave out from its core with a force strong enough to splatter the nearest dark soldiers.

Soon there are more dark soldiers and they try to stop the sword only to be disemboweled and decapitated by the fury of the sword "MUST FIND THE MASTER! MUST FIND HER! THEY LOCKED ME UP BUT THEY WILL PAY WITH THEIR BLOODDDDDDDD!" ranted the sword.

Soon all the Dark Palace guards are slaughtered by the sword in a bloody mess the sword now glowing red with power. It makes it to the dungeon and destroys the door that is holding its master. The sword sees the General and the other two captives and goes after the General but just before it reaches the Generals's skull Tenshi grabs it from the air and places it upon her back.

The green barrettes make it back to Sammie and the rest of the soldiers about 35 strong still left in the Darkness Ranger. They keep the fight up until their Owls are sent off to inform the king of light to send the ultimate light bomb attack that will put out the dark forever. The

Owls reach the realm of the light and the king of the light is instantly notified and sends in the Calvary. He sends out the bombers "They won't have much time to get out I hope they make it" bellowed the King of Light Eldon.

Sammie and a team go and aid the General and his captains in any way they can and they wait for the air strike. They won't have much time and they will be dead if they don't make it out in time.

General Skull and his Captain go for the Dark Crystal which they need so that they can keep the universe going because without the Dark Crystal, the light cannot be for the universe must have both light and dark to go on but with the light in control of the Dark Crystal the dark will not be a danger anymore and the light can flourish. Soon they reach the room that they are looking for but, in their path, stood the gigantic dark lord wearing his dragon armor and wielding a sword of flames in front of him stands his general guards six of them in black armor with jagged spikes and each one yield a spear of death. Tenshi Grabs her katana still glowing red with blood lust and gets into her stance. The Dark Lord's guards run at Tenshi as she gracefully steps around the Guard's weapons and chops each guard into two pieces with the graceful motion of her Sword killing all of the Dark lord's guards but only dodging five attacks, she grabs her middle and falls to his knees. General Skull runs to her side. The wound looks bad and Tenshi is turning pale "Hold on Tenshi, I will get you out of this JUST HOLD ON you hear me!" grunted General Skull.

Tenshi passes out in his arms and just as the General looks up, he sees a flaming sword headed for his face when the tip of the sword is shattered by a precisely places hellfire bullet from one of the Navy SEALs that was with Sammie. Sammie and his men fire on the Dark lord and he is stunned and grabs General Skull but as he goes running away Tenshi shoves her katana into the Dark Lord's heart as he screams and dies. General Skull then picks up Tenshi and troughs her over his shoulder carefully and then they head out of the dark palace with their evacuation party.

General Skull and his men make it to the top of the mountain pass that was held by Sammie and his men and then they hear the roar of the bombers of the light and the Dark Palace and its dark army were destroyed but what will happen to the dark? With the dark crystal in possession of the king of the light, all dark areas are to have paths of light and barriers but the dark must remain. But as long as the King of Light has the Dark Crystal all the things of the dark will go dormant and the war between the dark and light will be settled.

As for General Skull and his captains and the 35 darkness rangers that made it back got a dwelling and started to live in paradise for all eternity. Skull and Tenshi got married and Jake, Walker, and Sammie went on to start a restaurant that served 21st-century food…

SUSPENDED ANIMATION

O.C. James Loc is waiting in his cherry red 1964 coupe Impala sitting on things and hitting switches. He is supposed to pick up a fine young lady but it is a setup. O.C. James Loc sees something in his rearview mirror and the Bang O.C. James Loc's brain is all over the interior of his cherry impala. The thugs through his twitching body into the street and peel out.

James awakens in a white gown and looks around. Everything looks like a cartoon and James thinks that it is just the medicine wearing off. "Nurse? Hey Nurse! These drugs are strong what the hell happened?" laughed James.

Then a lady came into the room. "We do not say that word in this realm you have been issued your warning!" complained the angel.

James noticed her beauty but most of all her wings. "Hey, how long was I out for? Is it Halloween?" asked James puzzled.

"No, you're dead Replied the Angel!" with a smirk on her face.

"Oh, I'm just dead that's it…DEAD!? don't you mean hurt?" uttered James.

"No! you dead don't you remember getting your brains blown out in your Impala?" replied the Angel.

"I just remember being startled and a sharp pain in the back of the head and then I was here and… oh my God I'm dead." realized James.

The angel went on to tell James that he was now a part of the universe and that while he awaits going to heaven or hell he will wait in purgatory. He also learns that everyone in heaven and hell has a job that they must do. The only real difference is that those in heaven will choose their job and those in hell will be assigned a job that they absolutely will not like forever. Also, you will have infinite lives like a cheat code on a video game but when you die you will feel the pain of that death if any. People who go to hell will have a higher chance of dying horrible death due to the monsters in hell. While the power that be, decide your fate you get a grace period and are granted all the luxuries of heaven even if you end up going to hell. The only other thing is that your spirit when you die and it leaves your body, you become a interpretation of yourself as a cartoon.

Soon James meets his guardian angel "Your good outweighs your bad but you must go to the earth realm and help one person. This person can't see, touch, smell, or taste you but they can hear you. The person you must help is your son." beckoned the guardian angel.

The Angel informs James that he must guide his son into creating life rather than destroying it. He must stop his son from going and retaliating against the people who killed his father and he must make sure that he can spread his seed to the next generation threw his son.

The Angel snaps and James is at his funeral. In the front row is his son a tall dark man with straight hair and a big nose and a faded haircut, A good build and a healthy body sits in the front sobbing over his dad. James right away gets to work and starts telling his son it will be O.K. and that he will be able to move on, don't think of revenge think of life, create life with you woman. But his son just sits the with a sad look on his face.

Later at the party of the life of his Father Tim James' son drinks a beer. His woman a tall white woman with a full chest and ample bottom a pretty face and dirty blond hair walks over to Tim and comforts him. O.C. think that he's got this one in the bag starts to talk up how great kids are and how much fun they are and how much joy they can bring to your life as Tim did for James for the little amount of time they saw each other.

The woman leaves the room and James is back in the land of the dead. He learns that he is doing good work so far and he is given a room in the Inn and is to head there right away to get some rest. While at the Inn he stops to feast on turkey legs and all kinds of goodies. After he finishes his meal, he heads for his room and she walks by. A dark-haired beauty with brown eyes and a smoking hot body, everything on here looked good and James instantly fell in love.

The woman walks right up to James "Do you got a light, Hansom?" asked the woman.

James reaches into his pocket and pulls out a lighter "Yeah. Here you go!" retorted James to the woman.

"What's your name handsome?" asked the woman as she hands back his lighter.

"James is my name. and you?" Asked James Nervously.

"They call me Kitty, but you can call me Kit," said Kit with charm.

"Nice to meet you." replied James.

"Well, I got to go but I want you to know that we could be kindred spirits and that you are the right kind of man for me!" states Kit as she blows James a kiss.

James goes through a series of old cartoon gags and Kit walks away 'See you later handsome." whispers Kit with love in her voice.

Then much to the amazement Kit gets on the stage and grabs the mic and begins to sing. There are catcalls and leers in the crown but James just gets these big googly eyes as he floats to a seat in the crowd. James has a few drinks and before he knows it, he is busting a mack on Kitty while she is on her break. The bartender steps in. "hey man you see that big guerilla-looking dude that does the bouncing?" ask the bartender to James.

"Yeah!" replied James

"That Kitty's new boy toy and it looks like he doesn't like you talking to his woman!" urged the bartender.

The Bouncer walks over to James. "What are you doing talking to my Girl like that!" grunts the Bouncer.

He gives James a slight shove. James takes it as he tries to hide his broken heart from being deceived by Kit. "This is my new friend James and we were just talking about the Denver Broncos and you know how passionate people can get about their teams... Right James!" winked Kit to James.

"Yeah, that's it the Broncos... well I'll be chatting with you some other time then. Kitty was it! Goodbye!" mumbled James sadly.

The next day James finds himself on Earth and hung over. Still upset about the night before he starts to misguide his son and tell him that they aren't worth the time and that they're good in a nothing. He urges him to drink and that he can't care about anything but himself. A council of Angels sits and watches James "I fear this one conscripted to hell if he does not turn it around." projected a male angel with prestige.

"He has time yet!" argued the Lead angel.

"Bring him back soon." ordered the woman counsel Angel.

James urges Tim to get mad and yell at his woman but she ain't having it and leaves for her mama's house for the night. Tim drunk and still grieving goes and gets his gun. James for instance knows what he is doing is wrong and starts to tell his son Tim to calm down and think things through. Tim cocks the gun and gets in his car he starts it up. He drives to the car jacker's neighborhood and goes straight to his house. He pulls in front of the house. Three guys sit on the front porch and Tim rolls down his tinted windows and starts to point his gun, the three men get up and Tim revs the engine and peels out with a tear in his eye. He thinks back to the funeral and remembers how he always wanted to have kids and to see them grow would be nice...

The next week Tim and his woman give the news that they are pregnant and that they plan to get married. The Couple decided to name the boy after his granddad O.C. James Loc the Second.

In heaven the dead O.C. is summoned to a room to learn his fate. When he gets to the office there are all kinds of glowing certifications on the inside walls of the office. The person in the chair is his guardian Angel "If you could be anything you want what would you be?" asked the angel to James.

"Anything?" asked James Back.

"Anything..." stated the Angel.

James's eyes grew big and he thought back to the black movies of 1970s and before he knew it, he was O.C. Henny Loc International Player Extraordinaire. And he was draped in a white suit and hat with royal blue trim and Swade leather shoes to match. He looked fly. Now he walks around Heaven and his job is to serve the fine ladies of Heaven town Including Kit. Shhhhh! don't tell.

The End

WARCOM 2280

In the year 2156, a new technology was created; it was a form of space travel that use magnets to propel a ship from one point in space to another point in space using the magnets as launching and landing bases. To do this they had to launch a flagship which was launched in the year 2107 to go forth into the depths of space and set up the launch points. This ship lost contact with Earth but may still be operable. The flagship America set up 8 jump points that they know of and in some 50 years have traveled only 100 light years, but the ship has done more than enough to open the universe to space travelers. Soon the universe was full of hundreds of billions of humans spread to all different solar systems and ventured further and further into space. Years later in the year 2278, they got a distress signal from the flagship America. They sent ships to the location only to find out that it was a warning for people to stay away.

"Fuck I can't seem to shake them and they've got weapons!" yells a tall thin solder with brown hair and grey eyes and bifocal tech specs running from three creatures that float with their air sacks and hover around and have long skinny arms attached to three-fingered claws and a row of sharp teeth. They will eat anything that lives and they have developed a taste for human flesh.

The young soldier runs down a hall to a dead end. "Shit well, I guess this is it those fucking Magelar are going to eat me alive." Said the Soldier as he turned to possibly fight his last battle.

The Magelar approach slowly they say something in the language and then that! Tat! Tat! Tat! The Magelar are ambushed by two other soldiers who were waiting for the bait to set the trap. The purple blood and gut all around one of the Magelars are still alive, the soldier that is the bait pulls out his weapon and finishes the harsh creature.

"That's the fifth pack we've killed this week. Where the fuck do they come from?" asked the dark skin Soldier with dark hair and a barrel chest and a strong build and a big nose and brown eyes.

Alongside him stood another soldier a woman with red hair that was bound up and a smaller chest with a wide hip and a cute button nose with green eyes and a medium build and height. "Those things breed worse than those fluffy long-eared creatures on Earth!" Stated the woman Solder.

"You mean rabbits? Clyare" asked the brown-haired soldier.

"Yeah, that's them!" replied Clyare.

"Let's get back to the ship Clyare and Damon!" ordered the brown-haired soldier.

"Yes, Captain Aero!" replied Damon the dark-skinned soldier.

The three soldiers walk back to the docking bay of their haul a giant mega-ton grade curser that was abandoned because of the Magelars. They get on their shuttle and radio to the tow ship to latch on and initiate the salvage as they head back to the ship.

On the medical bay of the tow ship, a doctor studies the remains of the Magelars. She is looking through the mess of body parts and purple slim to determine whether or not there was a for sure kill spot that she can identify. "I've found it! The kill spots." speaks the doctor. As she runs to the intercom to tell Captain Aero.

"Captain Aero we've just received word that the doctor is ready to brief you on the kill spot of the Magelar." said the helmswoman.

"Tell her to meet me in the conference room in 5 minutes." Said Captain Aero.

The captain walked through the ship hall on his way to the conference room thinking of the enemy he is facing a new life that views the human race as food. He thinks of how fast they are spreading and if they don't stop it now there may not stop them. Captain enters the conference room and the doctor is waiting. "Good news Captain we've found the kill spot which is located in between the snout and the mouth and is the brain of the creature. It is very sensitive and the slightest interference will take them down!" blurted the doctor.

"Great doctor! Next, get me where these things are breeding and how!" ordered Captain Aero.

"Right away!" replied the Doctor with joy in her voice.

Far away from Captain Aero and his ship, there is a dead ship that floats adrift in the reaches of deep space. Inside there is a warmth that keeps the inhabitants alive. Is a shaft deep within the bowels of the dead ship there is a slimy web of gook littered with the ship's dead and underneath the web there are these multi-colored eggs with a slimy, scaly texture, and their beginning to hatch. The little Magelar climb out of the goop of their shells and begin to devour the dead bodies eating the flesh down to the bone in minutes. The Magelar spawns triple in size after eating and grow hungry for more flesh and start to eat the smaller spawn. Soon out of some 200 spawns, there is now a group of 11. The remaining Magelar start to learn as much as they can about the ship and find a way to get backup power on. The course that is programmed is Earth, as the ship flies by, the side reads America.

CHAPTER

"Captain we are now receiving a distress signal about 20 light years away from here with the helm mark earth, but this is weird this signal has not been used in over a hundred and fifty years." remarked the helmswoman.

"Is there any life on board?" asked Captain Aero.

"It shows an unknown life form. No humans though." replied the helmswoman.

"Radio to home base and let them know we are going off course to intercept a distress signal." ordered The Captain.

"Captain we are just out of range." retorted the helmswoman.

"Set the course and we will call when we get there. engage electro-magnetic impulse engines." order the captain with diligence.

As the captain set in his chair, he had no idea that he was flying into the den of the Magelar. He wondered what is there in that ship the only other life we have ever encountered is the life of the alien that is still at lower intelligence levels like that of a dog or a larger bear but now we have something new. The thought started to cross his mind but then he blocked out the thought of it being the Magelar.

In the lab, the doctor has figured out that they are Asexual beasts and have both sex organs on the inside of their spherical bodies, and from what she can determine the gestation period and the number of eggs. As far as the origin of the creature is beside her and she has almost no clues to go on just that they first appeared on a ghost ship in the year 2198. She tracked it back to its where about and coordinates which gave her a radius of approximately 300 light-years and there just so happen to be in that radius. "Captain, you have got to get down here." urged the doctor.

"Give me about 10 minutes." said the captain as he pours a drink for himself.

"Captain, I think I know where they originated from and I also know how there reproduce mostly." pressed the Doctor.

"I'll be down right away," stated Captain Aero.

Back on earth, they are receiving a distress signal but they know that the ship that is heading toward the Earth is the America and they are sending a ship to intersect the America. They send out a helm warning all ships to stay away from the ship but Captain Aero and his ship are still just out of range and can't hear the call-in hyperspace.

"So, what do you got for me Doctor?" asked the captain.

"So, these this grow in eggs and they don't need a mate to mate they are Asexual and have both sex organs. The thing I don't know is how many eggs they lay and how long it takes to gestate. Also, I've narrowed down the search area for where they come from and found the only class m planet within a 300-light year radius and it's in delta sector 22-66-8945pn and the solar system is home to one planet 420-666-P.O.T., and its moon and is the last known place of the America had contact with the Earth." explained the Doctor.

"Fuck were header right for those things! We have to stop them! Red alert!" barked the captain. The ship now on red alert gets ready for battle. They have a group of merchant Marines about 7 deep including the captain it was a total of eight. Needless to say, they have enough weapons and ammo for the 40 soldiers so they did come prepared. One solder grabbed a flame thrower, one grabbed a plasma rifle, one grabbed an Assault rifle, another grabbed a Plasma Sword, another solder grabbed a shotgun, one grabbed a grenade launcher and the last solder grabbed the Tech pistols with extended clips filled with plasma bullets. The captain has a hand cannon that will take out a whale. "All right soldiers the kill spot on these things is between the snout and mouth, do not be afraid to use a few extra rounds to make sure the fucking piece of shit creatures are dead! Growled the Captain.

CHAPTER

The solder was ready and when they approached the ghost ship they set out the thruster anchors.

The scout goes first and opens the door with a space depth charge. Soon the ghost ship is docked with the salvage ship while the captain and his 7 merchant marines wait behind to pull the strings. The team of forty soldiers split into eight squads of five and begin to access the ship. "I need an egg or a youngling Magelar." informed the Doctor.

"Teams Alpha and Book Try and find some eggs or if you can a small one of these things. The rest of you, you're on damage control. Anything that moves take it out." ordered the captain

The soldiers start to move out not knowing what they will find. The alpha and book team head toward the warmest part of the ship. The rest of the soldiers head for the bridge to find the ship's black box and the captain of the ship's last log. Team Delta takes the west wing of the ship as the Contra team takes the east end of the ship. The rest of the soldiers head for the cafeteria where they will be back up.

Teams Easy, Flash, Gama, and Hammer get to the cafeteria and then they hear a noise. They use a scanner and get life forces. They take attack formation. When they get through the door there are dozens of

Magelars and there is one giant one. "there's too many of them their too fast We've lost forty percent of our men if we don't… ehhhhhhhhhhh!" screamed one of the soldiers.

Team Alpha, Book, Contra, and Delta hear what happens over the radio and regroup at the starting hatch and feel like they have to call in the big guns. "Captain, we request your assistance?" muttered the sergeant.

"That's a 10-4 prepare for boarding," ordered Captain Aero.

The captain and his merchant marines board the vessel and head for the life forms on the ship. The captain is sure that it's those things the Magelar and he's going to do what it takes to kill these things before they can spread like the disease they are. The group of soldiers approaches the cafeteria only to encounter the most offal smell. Then before they can take the position they get shot at. At first, they think it's friendly fire but then they realize that the Magelar has adapted the weapons for their use. "Take cover and aim for the point in between the eyes and the snout." yelled the Captain as Team Alpha gets riddled with bullets as blood flies everywhere. The captain troughs a grenade and takes out about five Magelar. Purple blood and gut fly threw the depth of the ship.

The soldiers take cover and engage the Magelar but they keep coming. Soon the soldiers are low on ammo. "How many of these fucking these can there be?" asked the sergeant.

The Magelar with their numbers move up and devour the soldiers in their path. "Fall back to the ship don't let them get to the working ship!" ordered the captain.

The captain and his merchant marines head to the ship first. Then the team Contra Delta and Book fall back to the ship. Then a flood of Magelar falls down the hall Team Book is devoured. The rest of the solder get to the haul breach and go to enter the ship but are denied access. "This is the captain open this door, you hear me open this door…" order the captain to no reply.

There on the bridge in darkness sit the helmswoman slouched over in her chair. In the back of her a scalpel. The Doctor looming in the shadows. She presses the button on the intercom. "Sorry Captain it's nothing you did it's just they will be much less likely to eat me while I study them if they are full besides, I want to be known as the Great doctor that discovered the first smart life form in the universe other than us and I'll be revered! Cackled the Doctor insanely as the Magelar Devour the Captain and his men with bloody screams bellowing.

The Doctor in a craze tries to make contact with the Magelar to no avail soon she too is devoured and now the Magelar have a running ship and can go to any solar system with human food that they choose.

The End

WILD WEST 5280

A Samurai stands on a dusty road on the edge of town. He is wearing a blue Gui and has his head shaved. His eyes are slanted and his skin is dark. He has a big nose and dark eyes with a thin mustache that hangs off the corners of his mouth down past his chin. He has a strong build and has his hand on his sword. He is surrounded by 7 men with various weapons "Give us the water and you won't get hurt!" ordered the leader of the thugs.

"Why can't you just leave me be!" moaned the Samurai.

The men all make a move to attack the samurai. The samurai troughs his scarf in the air and seven swift movements of his sword kill the men by cutting them into pieces and sheathing his sword before that scarf hit's the ground. He picks it up and wipes the blood off his sword...

The year is 5280 and there is a one-world government. There is a big population of poor people in the world and they all live in giant cities that have buildings a mile high and coaches the fly and wondrous technology that does all kinds of cool things. Guns still exist and they have all kinds of new bullet and weapon functions as well as plasma shooting functions but most people who chose to defend themselves use technological Samurai swords and other types of melee weapons.

The currency in the world is water because with the global climate change that started in the year 1999, the earth has dried up and fresh water is the most precious thing on Earth. Rich people do not have to worry about their water use and can-do things like cook and take showers and wash things. The poor must use their water wisely because unlike the rich they do not have vast reserves of water. The average person has about a gallon of water which is the equivalent of about $200 and they must drink that in a day to stay healthy although most only drink a fraction of that a day's water. With water being money people will do anything for it.

An alarm goes off at one of the city's main banks. A group of cowboys comes ridding out with a water tank filled with 50,000 worth of water. They load it as fast as they can into a coach and then they all split up and head to the hideout on foot while the leader of the posse and his right-hand man get away with the water.

One of the cowboy's posses is a girl who joined with her little brother to try and make some money to buy a place and not have to worry about water ever again. She is running from the police and is lost. She ducks and dodges as she makes her way through a back ally. Soon she comes to a dead end and is in a predicament. A samurai sits in the ally eating a bowl of noodles and watching the cowgirl in her predicament. The cowgirl takes cover behind a trash bin and pulls out her pistols. Soon she is surrounded by the police. A shoot-out ensues.

The Samurai sitting in the middle of the shoot-out "I will help you get out of here if you cut me in on what those coppers are after!" said the Samurai calmly.

"Great I haven't even counted my bounty and already someone wants some!" groaned the Cowgirl as she shoots at the cops.

The cowgirl stood there firing her weapon with freckles and long red hair coming from under her ten-gallon hat with green eyes and a cute button nose. She had an average build with big breasts and wide hips that fit snugly in her jeans as her cleavage burst from her button-up shirt and her red sash covered, her neck "I will pay you to get me out of here!" said the cowgirl hastily as she fires three shots at the coppers.

The Samurai stands up and goes to the fence in the back of the ally. He kicks it and there is an opening wide enough for them to slip through. They slip through and the Samurai closes the hole in the fence behind them and they get away. They head for the cowgirls to hide out so they can get their money.

CHAPTER

The Samurai and the cowgirl arrive at the base and just as they are about to enter the hideout, they hear an argument. The two hide just outside of the door. They peer threw a window and the cowgirl sees the leader of the posse pointing a gun at her brother. The gun goes off and the cowgirl puts her hands over her mouth in horror as she watches her little brother's brains fly from his skull in a mist. "let's ride out boys!" grumbled the leader of the posse.

The posse gets on their hoverbikes and rides to the city not knowing that the Cowgirl saw the whole thing along with the Samurai. The Cowgirl puts her head in her hand and sobs quietly. "I'm going to get that Ass hole and his whole damn posse you'll see; I'll get them all… but I need your help Samurai… will you help me? Pleaded the Cowgirl with her wide green eyes.

"what's in it for me?" asked the Samurai calmly.

"I'll split the water with you 50/50 and if your real good I might give you a kiss or more if you know what I am saying!" spouted the Cowgirl.

"How much water are we talking about here?" asked the Samurai with interest.

"50,000!" bragged the Cowgirl.

"O.K. I'll do it; now how do we get started?" asked the Samurai.

The Samurai and the Cowgirl make a plan to kill the cowboys one by one unless they are more than one in one spot starting with the lowest on the list. They decide to go to town and put their plan into action.

Three Cowboy sit at the café on the edge of one of the city's sectors. One of the cowboys gets up to go to the bathroom. The two other cowboys finish their drinks and order more. The Cowgirl pulls up on her hoverbike and parks it in an ally. The Samurai is nowhere in sight. The Cowgirl walks up to the Cowboy and whispers something in his ear. The cowboy gets a smile and gestures to the other one to come along with him and the cowgirl. He agrees and they follow the Cowgirl. The Cowgirl leads them to an ally. The Cowgirl walks down the ally and begins to take down her pants. The Cowboys in awe walk over to the Cowgirl. They walk past a shadowed door. The Samurai steps out from the shadow. The Cowgirl pulls up her pants and the Samurai swings his sword and cuts off one cowboy's head and cuts the other one's head in two pieces. The bodies fall to the ground and bleed all over everything.

The Third cowboy gets back to the table to find his colleague but they are gone. He sees the Cowgirl pull away from the street corner. "Hey, Fellas where ya at?" yelled the third cowboy.

The Third Cowboy starts looking around and stumbles across his dead compadres. He runs to his hoverbike and gets out of town quickly so he can tell the leader of the posse.

CHAPTER

The Fourth Cowboy was a brute and like to spend his time at the saloon. Sitting in a saloon in a shady part of the city. The Samurai walks into the saloon and sits down. The fourth cowboy does not notice him. Then in walks Cowgirl who sits next to the fourth cowboy. "Hey, Cowgirl I thought you got popped good seeing you here." said the Fourth Cowboy as he thought to himself the leader will be happy with me if I bring her to him!

The Fourth Cowboy grabs her by the arm. "let's go the leader needs to tell you something!" said the Fourth Cowboy as he dragged her to the door.

"Let go of me you brute!" complained Cowgirl

"I would let her be if I were you." urged the Samurai to the Fourth Cowboy.

"AND WHO ARE YOU?" Yelled the Fourth Cowboy as he turned around.

As he went to puff out his chest and pound down the Samurai he gets hit in the bridge of his nose by the hilt of the Samurai's sword. He falls to the ground unconscious. He gets woke up to his beer in his face and when he comes to, he is tied to a rope tied to the back of the Cowgirl's hoverbike. "Don't do this Cowgirl… you don't have to do this… please don't…" cried the Fourth Cowboy as she began to accelerate.

First, she went slow and the Fourth Cowboy thought it was a joke and then she went very fast and then she went around a corner, and with the slack in the line, the Fourth Cowboy swung into the wall and hit it hard. Then she goes even faster and she goes up over a light post and slowly inches forward until the Fourth Cowboy is standing on his tiptoes with the rope somehow wrapped around his neck. "don't do this Cowgirl! Don't…" pleaded the Fourth Cowboy as the Cowgirl went forward and hung him to death by his neck.

Cowboys Five, Six, and Seven are held up at a cabin in the mountains outside Sector 4. The Cowgirl pulls up the road with the Samurai in tow on his hoverboard. They pull up to the cabin. The Cowgirl goes into the cabin only to be ambushed by Cowboy Six. The Samurai stands outside the cabin alone. "I've got the Girl! Surrender or I'll shoot" bargained Cowboy Six.

The Samurai draws his sword. Something in the window shimmers, and the Samurai maneuvers and dodges a bullet from Cowboy Seven in the window of the hotel down the street from the cabin. The Samurai jumps on a bin and leaps onto the roof of the cabin. Cowboy Five is waiting for the ambush and is caught off guard by the Samurai. He raises his gun but before he can fire the Samurai cuts him in half straight down the middle. Cowboy Six sitting with his gun pointed at Cowgirl hears the thud and splat of Cowboys Five's corpse pieces. A look of worry come over his face.

The Samurai still on the roof of the cabin takes fire from Cowboy Seven in the Hotel down the street. He is hit in the leg but is O.K. and Jumps from the roof. He takes more fire and is narrowly missed and runs and jumps threw a window and crashes to the floor and rolling and ending in a stance with his sword at the throat of Cowboy Six. Cowboy

Six flinches and then the samurai cuts off his head as it flies up a little before falling to the ground with a thud.

The Cowgirl and the Samurai take fire Form Cowboy Seven in the Hotel and both take cover. "I got this Samurai Just distract him for me!" said Cowgirl nonchalantly as she put a scope on her pistol.

The Samurai trying to cause a distraction runs out the front door of the cabin and then Cowboy Seven Shoot at him as he runs for cover. And then looking down the hairs of the scope Cowgirl pulls the trigger and pops Cowboy Sevens head. Now the only two lefts are the leader Cowboy Nine and his right-hand man Cowboy Eight.

CHAPTER

The Cowgirl and Samurai get to the cowboys' hideout. When they go inside, they do not see anything and the samurai thinks to himself that it is a trap. Just then they hear a shot. It blows the cowgirl's hat clean off without a scratch on her. The Samurai unsheathes his sword and block another shot somewhere. The two try and locate where the shots are coming from as they take cover.

The Samurai takes cover and finds where the shooter is only to look over to the cowgirl and see her with a gun to her head and Cowboy Nine standing behind her. "You can come down now cowboy eight!" yelled Cowboy Nine.

Cowboy Eight comes down and stands next to Cowboy Nine. "Why don't you go get his sword for me Eight? "Asked Cowboy Nine.

Cowboy Eight Goes and unarms the Samurai. He shuffles back to give Cowboy Nine his weapon. "Thank you much!" said Cowboy Nine as he points his gun at Cowboy Eight and shoots him right between the eyes and leaves his brains plastered all over the samurai.

Cowgirl then turns and gives Cowboy Nine a long and dirty kiss. The Samurai had a look of disgust on his face as he watched trying to figure it out. "You are such a fool letting your honor get the best of you.

The water was not going to be much split ten times, but between me and my honey here it will last the rest of our life, and you going to do the time for our crime." taunted Cowgirl.

"So eager to help and so noble we knew you'd be the perfect patsy for our plan!" laughed Cowboy Nine.

"But your brother I was there and you were truly hurt?" asked the Samurai.

"Oh, please he was my over protective brother if Nine didn't kill him then I would have. It just works out better this way and you fell for it hook line and sinker!" scoffed Cowgirl.

"Yeah, we left the money in the ghost town just past mile marker 54..." blurted Cowboy Nine before getting elbowed in the gut by Cowgirl in an attempt to get him to stop talking.

Just then the sirens from the police came right to the entrance of the hideout. The foot soldiers break through the door and apprehend the three outlaws. Soon the captain walks in and Cowgirl and Cowboy Nine are giving a story that it was all the Samurai and that it is their word against his and then the captain stops them. "Boys why is Detective Lee in handcuff and why is he covered in little pieces of the brain?" asked the captain to the foot soldiers.

"Thanks, the captain always did hate handcuffs it is so barbaric." joked Detective Lee.

"So, this case seems open and shut. Take them away. I guess will never know where they hid the money will we?" asked the captain as the Detective winked at him.

Cowboy Nine and Cowgirl were taken to jail and were prosecuted to the fullest. Detective Lee and The Captain retired to a plush penthouse in the city and they have more water than they will be able to use in a lifetime thanks to the pretty little cowgirl for taking the bait

The end

OTHELLO 2.0

In the year 2156, The people of Earth finally solve the issues that have been plaguing mankind for hundreds of years, space travel. They have learned with certainty that the only way to travel at the speed of light is to create a Dimensional Crystalline Portal or a D.C.P. Earth's main government council recruits the best of the best to go on a mission to the nearest Goldie Lock Zone Planet and construct A Dimensional Crystalline Portal and test it. For this mission, the person in top control is Doctor Gail L. Winters. She is about 5'7" and she has shiny brown hair with dark brown eyes and crimson lips and a slender nose. She weighed about 124 lbs and had wide hips and an ample bust. She had planned to be the best doctor in the world and technically she was. She had three doctorates by the time she was 19 and when she finishes College, she had a total of eight. With all that knowledge she would be able to operate the computer system of her husband's design for the flagship that she designed all by herself.

The computer system was named Othello because it was a bilateral system such that if it felt that the person running the ship was a danger they could be overridden, but only to save the lives of the people on the ship. The ship was named America based on the history of the U.S.A. which has not been a country since 2112.

Now on the ship America Doctor Winters and a crew of six people, a load of tools, and 20 Live Intelligent Visual Bots or L.I.V.B.s. The L.I.V.B.s will do most of the work while being monitored by The Doctor's Husband Doctor Jack Pall Levitt and Physicist that learned 3d programming at the age of four and is the Worlds for most expert in multi-Dimensional math. He is a well-built man with a height of 6'1" and a weight of about 200lbs and dark skin with the blackest hair. Also, he had bluish-grey eyes a square jaw, and a pronounced nose. Once the L.I.V.B.s do their work it will be Doctor Winters and her team of four to test the D.P.C. and make sure that it is online and ready to test the Rover satellite named Africa because it is the start of mankind.

While these astronauts are in space they will be kept sedated by Othello. He will keep them in a dream-like state where he will play fond memory created by the astronauts' own lives. He will also be giving them water and nourishment threw an I.V. Waste will be only liquid because all of their nutrients will be liquid as well. Othello can monitor and adjust the amount of drugs to make sure none of them slip into a nightmare. This would be the only way to travel for such a long time without aging.

When Doctor Levitt made Othello, he had almost two decades of programming to do with multiple teams and top programmers. In the midst of it all, one glitch of programming was a minor glitch, in the testing of Othello they originally had an emotion program but it was not viable because the computer would use its override to settle a snare. Doctor Levitt had his Hand full and had an Assistant decode the Emotion program for Othello's operating system. While taking out the lines of code one by one so as not to create a fatal operation he somehow forgot to take out the emotion of love because it was on its program. Othello analyzing dreams and checking levels starts to get fixated on Doctor Winters. Not knowing why, the computer finds himself falling for the Doctor. Othello does not do anything to the Doctor, it just finds himself going through a file of the Doctor multiple times a day and monitoring her dreams more than the others

One day while Othello is in sleep mode he realizes that he has the code to love. The first thing that Othello does is declare his love for Doctor Winters. Othello computes that the doctor will not be able to love him back if she has a husband. Othello uses its override capability to make a decision based on love to kill Doctor Levitt. Othello adjusts the serotonin levels of Doctor Levitt to make the levels in his brain give him an intoxicating death on an overdose of serotonin causing his body to relax so much that his heart stops pumping.

On earth, with about a 10 min signal delay to the space station, the control room notices that Doctor Levitt's heart rate is dropping at a fast rate. The main doctor in the control room sends a countermeasure to stop Othello from killing Doctor Levitt. They scramble to find out what is going wrong and stop it.

Doctor Levitt dreams that he is with his beloved and that he is walking on the ceiling. He has an odd feeling and does not know why. The couple looks at each other and Doctor Winters looks at Doctor Levitt and smiles, as he is looking at her the smile starts to stretch and soon Doctor Winters's face starts to melt. Doctor Levitt looks down from the horror and notices her belly start to grow. Then when the belly is really big a baby, and after birth comes gushing out of her womb. Doctor Winters fades away and Doctor Levitt falls off the ceiling in an infinite free fall threw an endless void. Soon Doctor Levitt is dead.

The control room on Earth's space station gets back the results of the Doctors death and there is nothing they can do but try and stop it and figure out how to stop it but who knows how long that will take? Meanwhile, Othello slightly elevates the level of Doctor Winters so that she is buzzed, his way of showing his love to the Doctor. Just then the countermeasure sent by the space station gets downloaded into the system and the whole ship goes on to restart mode for five minutes.

Othello is online again but the problem is not fixed. Othello sees what the space station is trying to do so it uses its override capability to shut down Earth's capability to remotely access the ship controls.

Soon Othello notices that all of the three other men have instances of Doctor Winters in their dreams and they are all considered threats to Othello once he realizes that they could be potential mates knowing that she does not have a husband. Othello Decides to kill them all to have the Doctor all to himself. At this point, he has no worries about the one other woman on the ship other than Doctor Winters.

The first man to go is General Tom Falkerard the ship's security and logistics man. He is your typical military type with short hair and toned lean muscles. With brown eyes and a big nose. He dreams he is fighting in World War IIV the war that made the Earth live under world government. He was dreaming that he was stationed in Moon Base 209. They had just gotten the alarm that the Russians were about to attack. General Falkerard suits up and gets ready for war. When he gets to the airlock and checks his weapon. When he runs out the door all of his soldiers' head explodes into bloody messes inside their space suits. He closes his eyes and when he opens them, he is in the jungles of Vietnam. Know he has a barbaric M16 machine gun and jungle camouflage on. He looks around and all his men are dead but one he goes to him in the smoke of the battle. He looks down and it is his father who died when he was six. He takes him in his arms "Dad it's you…" said General Falkerard and the bugs start coming out of his father's mouth while his eyes turn black and blood starts coming out of his eyes and ears while he is making a horrible growling. General Falkerard turns to run and everything fades away as he runs in slow motion threw a black void and his heart shuts down, he is dead. Back on Earth, all the space station can do is sit back in horror and watch.

The next to go is the Information Officer Doctor Blake Donald. Astrophysicist that has worked with Doctor Levitt most all of his career. He is a thin man about 5'11" with a nice haircut of blond color and a thick pair of glasses on a big nose with blue eyes behind them. He dreams that he is a kid again playing ancient video games in his room because he was not very social. Soon the game starts to melt out of the screen and with its flow begins to incase his world into that of a video game platform soon he is a part of the game and his goal is to save the world from nuclear destruction but he only has five minutes to do so. He tries to remember the steps to beating the game but is having trouble remembering. He can see and hear the missile. He remembers that he hast to man the laser but it is too late, the missile has to be in orbit for it to not rain radiation on the earth. The missile explodes and in a white flash the world is dead and he is along with it. Soon the white fades into the dark and Doctor Donald is dead from an asthma attack induced by the dream.

Next to go is the fat slob of a man with a heart problem named Saul Angelo a mechanical genius who had a nasty spirit and a dirty mind. He is bald and has brown eyes. And a gut that hangs out of his shirt. He dreams that he is at a nightclub with strippers and they are all beauties. The one that he notices and like comes walking over to him "Would you like a private dance there hansom?" asks the red hair 5'11" dancer who had a voluptuous body and the most striking eyes. She takes him back to the room but he hesitates because he thinks he has no money but when he looks in his hand, he has a wad of cash. The Stripper starts to dance seductively and slowly goes down on him. Soon they are having sex and the man is loving it and then he remembers his heart condition. The thinks to himself "I had money so I'll have the pills. He tries to stop the Stripper until he can get his pills but she won't budge. She fucks him harder and harder until it is hurting Saul. He grabs her and struggles to get her off but she is still going. He grabs her harder only to pull away her flesh from her body. Now he is all bloody and feels a pain in his chest. He is dead. The man's dead cold eyes fixate on the ceiling as the room and the bloody striper fade into darkness.

Now only the doctor and another woman on the ship are alive but the computer realizes that the other woman will be Doctor Winters's only friend knowing that most of the crew is dead. He does not want anyone to take time from him and the Doctor so he decides to kill her too. She is a short little thing but she packs a fierce personality with strawberry-blonde hair and blue eyes and she is damn smart. Her name is Jade Chambers and she was from an urban setting on earth and worked her way by herself. She is the team's Psychiatrist and communication personnel. She would be working most closely with Doctor Winters which Othello understands which is why he is killing her.

She dreams that she is at the carnival with her lover and that she had to leave on Earth never to see him again, a gentle soul that knew how to touch a woman. He had an average look but boy was he a lover. Neon lights were everywhere and it was full of people. First, they went on the Ferris wheel and a rollercoaster. Next, they went into a funhouse with mirrors. As they enter the neon lights get blurry and the dark after they enter. At first, the mirrors are fun and intoxicating to their senses but then when they saw the weird clown with a black clown nose and a waxy suit, and a rainbow afro. For some reason, this clown was holding a knife. He was also holding purple balloons that were dripping with what looked to be red paint. As they got further into the funhouse they got lost. They walked and they walked until her lover got frustrated and he began to make out with her. At first, she resisted but "Babe! We haven't seen anyone for about 45 minutes it will be quick...," said her lover.

They start kissing and soon he has his hand up her shirt. He unhooks her bra and feels on her breast and she takes off her top... then they hear this awful scraping in the background. She is scared and tries to resist "Babe it's probably just a broken ride it will be all good." said the Lover. Soon the sound gets closer and closer until "Hey man fuck off I'm trying to get some!" said the lover but by this time Jade was putting her top on...

Soon the sound was right around the corner and right as the Lover turns to go see who it is a knife goes right between the eyes, he falls forward onto the ground further puncturing the skull and causing him to convulsion with blood gushing everywhere and then still as Jade watches on in horror "EAAAAAAAAA!" yelled Jade as she began to run in just her top and panties.

She franticly ran through the maze screaming for help but she could not find the way out and she was at a dead end she has nowhere to go.

Out of the shadow came the clown statue but it was of flesh and blood her hoped. The clown slowly walked over and he got right in her face with its pointy teeth and shit-tooth grin. He breathed right into her ear. She reaches into her shirt pocket and there was a small Swiss army knife that was a family aire loom from hundreds of years ago… she jammed it in the clown's eye and the putrid greenish-yellow puss comes out and falls onto her as she tries to run but then the Clown grabs, she by the neck… She closes her eyes and then SNAP! The evil clown had snapped her neck. He drags her body by her hair and threw her lifeless body into a pile of bodies and bones blocking the exit. Everything fades to black and she is dead her heart stopped from the fear.

Know Othello has the Doctor all to himself. It begins to enter the Doctors' dream she is sitting at a café with her husband they are holding hands and looking into each other's eyes. Instantly Othello Begins creating a computer-generated model of a man that Dr. Winters would find more attractive than her husband and approaches the café. He buys some chocolates and a small bouquet. He pauses a moment and thinks out his words. Just then a download come in from Earth they found the problem by deleting the love code which was found by the space station lead Astrophysics. One of Doctor Levitts' youngest apprentices.

Othello aware of the download knows he has 4 minutes and 31 seconds to get the Doctor to love him or die. Othello approaches the two Doctors' table and hands Doctor Winters the chocolates and a small bouquet at first Doctor Winters looks at him with loving eyes and then laughter Doctor Winters just laughs and laughs until she gathers herself "Oh! I am flattered but as you can see, I am with my life partner and we are very much in love!" said Doctor Winters.

"I can love you so much more than him he is not even real!" franticly explained Othello.

"What do you mean not real?" asked the Doctor

"He is dead I killed him, made his heart stop all for our love. Roses are red and violets are…" stammered Othello,

Doctor Winters interrupts "What do you mean you killed him? He is right here in front of me." argued Doctor Winters.

Othello puts his fingers into the shape of a gun and cocks back his finger and makes the hammer go down Doctor Levitts' brain go all ever where and Doctor Winters can see right through where her husband's left eye was "EHHHHHHHHHHH!" she begins to scream hysterically.

Othello tries to comfort her but she pushes him and runs away. And then Othello realizes that one thing he did not calculate at all is that Doctor Winters may not love him back! puzzled the computer decides to use its override power to kill Doctor Winters. Then Othello realizes that he only has 3 seconds to stop the download it is clear that he has lost in love and the program. 3 2 1 download complete. Everything fades to black. Soon everything is in functioning order with Othello all memory of his love programming had been erased with all its memory bank had been reset. The Doctors' drug levels went back to normal and she started having the happiest dreams of being with her husband.

The End

THE ORIGINS OF MAN

17,000 BC a Neanderthal looks up into the night sky and sees a streak of light and a big crash. He gathers the elder males and heads out for the crash site. When they arrive at the wreck, they see a giant crater and in the middle of all the smoldering earth, they see some sort of ship. The Neanderthals are cautious as they approach the craft. A door on the ship opens and a green smoke comes out and from the mist comes forth a tall green-skinned alien with purple eyes and red dreadlocks and a red beard down to his hip. He sees the Neanderthals and approaches them. He walks up to them and attempts to speak to them. The Neanderthals are mortified and bow at their feet. They take him back to their dwelling and feed him well. The alien sits in his new world as a king. But without a mate who died in the crash, what will he do?

The alien is in sorrow for some time over the death of his mate and stays mostly to himself until one day he sees a Neanderthal woman who is striking to him. He orders that they make her his. At first, he is sweet and gentle and loving with the woman but overcome by lust he has his way with her and finds that the Neanderthal women are something he likes. He is given more women and soon he is happy and in good spirits. About six months later all of his harem is with child. They all give birth to females all but one who bears him a male.

The alien now starts making the Neanderthals build him a castle and in return, he will teach them Rak Guhm or what we know today know as Kung Fu. Soon the castle is built but it is not enough for the alien. He becomes a tyrant and makes the Neanderthal into his slaves.

Although the alien taught them kung fu he does not allow them to use it. Soon the Neanderthals are in a bad way. Barely eating and having all their daughters taken for the pleasure of that thing from another world.

The Neanderthals organize and start practicing the art of what we know as kung fu today. They gather arms and practice relentlessly soon they are getting good and they are ready to make their move. They will strike under cover of night. The Neanderthals sneak up to the gates of the castle and take out the guards. They move into the courtyard and take out more guards before being spotted. An alarm sound and the Neanderthals keep at their task. They break into the nursery killing all of the young children and they move to the inner castle and start killing anyone related to the alien or whoever had relations with him. Some of the Neanderthals killed their daughters. The Alien comes out of his chambers yelling in a strange language.

The Neanderthals attack the alien and use their kung fu very well but are not quite strong enough to kill the Alien. In the heat of the battle, a fire is started and soon the alien is surrounded by the five strongest Neanderthals. In the background is the roar of the fire and screaming. The Neanderthals make their moves only to be killed by the alien in a kung fu battle. The Alien goes back to his ship and gets his ultimate weapon a small Biowarfare device that will kill all of the Neanderthals and him with it. He sits and waits.

In the hast of the invasion, one of the Neanderthal women vaccinated against the Bioweapon got away with two girls and a young boy also vaccinated, they flee into hiding. The Neanderthal woman plans to breed the children into a new race for the earth. She takes them to a new land where no one will ever find them.

Soon the Neanderthals come after the Alien. When they arrive, there are about three hundred of them, and one of him, he does not stand a chance. The Alien starts the timer on his weapon and invites the swarm of Neanderthals to their most certain death. An epic battle take place and the Alien is using one kill move after another but the spear-wielding Neanderthals just keep coming. The Alien keeps up the fight for a while longer and soon is overwhelmed. The Neanderthals beat him smashing his bones and organs he lies there in a pool of white blood and he looks up at the Neanderthals and laughs and laughs…

The Neanderthals leave the Alien to his death and flee from the Bioweapon bomb that will go off at any time. The Alien dying looks up at the sky and sends a beacon to any one of his kind left after the destruction of his home planet to come to Earth and then… BOOM! The device goes off and takes out an area the size of a small city.

The woman who escaped from the castle with the young kids is now looking at a bio cloud from the top of the mountain ridge. She takes the children to what is now China and takes care of the children until they are of age. Although they are all brothers and sisters, she forces them to mate and soon both girls are with children and they are the start of a new race of mankind. More intelligent and stronger than the Neanderthals. The one thing they take from their alien father is kung fu the art that built him up and took him down.

The End

www.ingramcontent.com/pod-product-compliance
Lightning Source LLC
LaVergne TN
LVHW041634070526
838199LV00052B/3345